DATE			

THE 24-HOUR GENIE

Here are some other
Redfeather Books from Henry Holt

The Class with the Summer Birthdays
by Dian Curtis Regan

*Cory Coleman, Grade 2
by Larry Dane Brimner

*The Fourth-Grade Four
by Marilyn Levinson

*Max Malone and the Great Cereal Rip-off
by Charlotte Herman

Max Malone Makes a Million
by Charlotte Herman

*Monstra Vs. Irving
by Stephen Manes

*Snakes Are Nothing to Sneeze At
by Gabrielle Charbonnet

*Something Special
by Emily Rodda

Stargone John
by Ellen Kindt McKenzie

213 Valentines
by Barbara Cohen

*Weird Wolf
by Margery Cuyler

**Available in paperback*

Lila Sprague McGinnis

THE 24-HOUR GENIE

Illustrated by Michael Sours

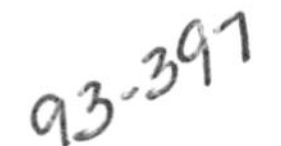

A Redfeather Book
Henry Holt and Company / New York

Published by Henry Holt and Company, Inc.,
115 West 18th Street, New York, New York 10011.
Published in Canada by Fitzhenry & Whiteside Limited,
195 Allstate Parkway, Markham, Ontario L3R 4T8.

Library of Congress Cataloging-in-Publication Data
McGinnis, Lila Sprague.
The 24-hour genie / by Lila Sprague McGinnis ;
illustrated by Michael Sours.
(A Redfeather book)
Summary: Fourth-grader Andrew thinks he has it made when he finds a genie that can grant his every wish, until he realizes that each wish lasts for only twenty-four hours.
[1. Wishes—Fiction. 2. Magic—Fiction.] I. Sours, Michael, ill. II. Title. III. Title: Twenty-four-hour genie. IV. Series.
PZ7.M16775A15 1990
[E]—dc20 89-77786

ISBN 0-8050-1303-2 (hardcover)
10 9 8 7 6 5 4 3 2
ISBN 0-8050-1845-X (paperback)
10 9 8 7 6 5 4 3 2 1

Published in hardcover in 1990 by
Henry Holt and Company, Inc.
First Redfeather paperback edition, 1991

Designed by Victoria Hartman
Printed in the United States of America

Contents

THE 24-HOUR GENIE

1

A Jinn Called Jo

Uncle Donald stowed a brown box in Andrew's closet. Then he hugged the whole family, waved good-bye, and headed north to the Arctic.

Andrew went upstairs to his room and his bats.

The red bat hung upside down far over his head in the corner. The brown bat flew on a wire over his bed. Uncle Donald had brought them last year for Andrew's science project.

Andrew pushed at the brown bat to set it swinging, and then he pushed at Uncle Donald's box.

He *did not* look inside.

But—the lid bounced sideways, and a bottle rolled out.

Andrew grabbed it.

Just shoe polish. As he put it back, he saw two eyes peering out from inside the bottle.

One eye winked.

No way, said Andrew to himself. I did not see eyes.

He pushed the lid down on the box.

Then he took it off again. He took the bottle out of the box and out of the closet and put in on his desk.

The eyes were gone. Andrew opened the bottle and waited for a puff of smoke or a swirl of mist, but nothing happened.

Except, a small blue creature sat on top of Andrew's dictionary, blowing at itself.

Andrew sat down. He was surprised, for he hadn't known he was sleeping. He leaned on the chair and stared at his guest.

The small person turned a bright shade of pink, and then blew itself violet, and then red. . . .

Andrew watched and thought. His uncle collected the strangest things; this might be *real*! He pinched himself on the arm three times. It hurt three times.

He shook his head, but the little person did not go away. I must be wide awake, Andrew thought. Out loud, he said, "I liked the blue suit best."

The creature stopped blowing.

"A common color," it said.

"But I like it," said Andrew. "Genies come out of bottles, so are you a genie? And since I let you out, am I your master?"

The small person gave one last blow, turning himself

into a summer-sky shade of blue. His face was round and rosy, and his dark curls sparkled in the light from the window. He was six inches tall.

Of course, maybe he was a she.

He said it didn't matter. "My name is Jo."

"That's no help." Andrew swung the chair around and put his elbows on the desk so he and the little person were looking eye to eye. "Is it short for Joseph or Josephine?"

"Jo is short for . . . Jo. Where I come from, I'm known as a jinn."

"And jinn means genie, right?" Andrew held tight to the back of the chair. He had never met a genie before, and he felt a little scared. "Where do you come from?" he asked.

"I know where I come from. The question is, Where am I right now?"

"My house," said Andrew. "120 Oxford Street, Bentley, Ohio, the United States of America."

"Ohio? America?" Jo's arms flew up, and the whole top of him shrunk and dissolved into the bottom of him. He looked like a blue puffball sitting on the red-and-white book.

Andrew took off his glasses and put them on again. He tapped out the first line of "My Country 'Tis of Thee"

on the edge of his desk. Then, just as he decided to blow at the puffball, Jo's small face appeared, and then his arms, and in a moment he was back to six inches.

"America is a long way from home," he said. He tugged at one blue shoe until the toe curled. "So be it." He sighed and pulled the other toe.

"Are you sad?"

"A little bit, I think," said Jo. "The tall man—"

"My uncle, you mean."

"Short, curly yellow hair? Wears tired-blue pants and talks a lot? Name of Donald?"

Andrew grinned. "That's him. They're called blue jeans. I wear them too."

Jo leaned far over and studied Andrew's pants. "Not silky like mine. Your toes don't curl either."

"That's true," said Andrew. Thank goodness, he added to himself.

"Is your uncle coming back soon?"

"You can't ever tell about Uncle Donald. He's never where you expect him to be. And I bet he didn't mean to leave you behind."

They both thought about that. Then Jo said, "Well, he wouldn't be back tonight, anyhow," and Andrew said, "No, he wouldn't."

"Are you called Andy?" asked the genie.

"No one ever does. I don't know why. Just Andrew,"

he said. "I thought genies were great huge ugly things."

Jo sat down and crossed his legs. "We come in all sorts and sizes. You aren't like every other human boy, are you?"

"I'll say I'm not. For one thing, I'm shorter than everyone else in my class."

"I'm a little short too," Jo said.

"But I'm smarter than everyone else."

"I'm smart too." The genie slapped his knees. "About being my master," he said. "Is that important? I thought we might be friends, instead. I'm tired of always being bossed, Andrew. I've been wanting a real friend for hundreds of years."

"Me too," said Andrew. He took off his glasses and polished them while he thought. Before David had moved away, right after Christmas, they had been best friends. They had liked the same things, and they had done everything together. He had never wanted to be with anyone else, no matter how his mother had fussed at him to play with other kids.

Now he felt stranded. There wasn't anyone he knew who liked what he liked. He could use a friend, all right.

Andrew put his glasses on again and said there was just one thing. . . .

"When I say hop into the jar, you'll have to hop," he

said. "Fast!" he added, thinking of his sister, who always burst into his room without knocking.

"I will! That's an unbreakable rule anyhow."

"Well then—I can use a friend too. My best one moved to Hartford." Andrew held out his index finger. "We'll be good friends, Jo. Let's shake on it. Can you do magic?"

"Magic!" The genie jumped up and down, pulling Andrew's finger along. "Try me!" he cried. "I'll blow you up something wonderful! Just tell me what you want."

"*Anything* I want?"

2

No Problem!

Andrew knew what he wanted.

"Two inches," he exclaimed. "I want to be two inches taller."

"That's tricky," Jo said. "We'll talk about it later."

Andrew shrugged; he hadn't really expected that the genie could do it.

"Well, then, my homework. We're going to the movies in a little while, and I'm supposed to be doing my math homework, not talking to you. *If* I really am talking to you."

"Certainly you are talking to me. Did you think you were dreaming?" The genie gave a sigh that was twice the size of himself. Then he said people always thought they were dreaming. "You are awake," he said. "I guarantee it."

"In that case, can you do my homework for me?"

"What grade are you in?" asked Jo.

"Fourth."

"No problem!" said the genie. He blew a soft gust of air toward the paper Andrew had pulled from his book bag. "Will that do?"

Andrew saw twenty multiplication problems done in pencil, the numbers written just as he would have written them. All three-digit numbers, too.

"Wow!" he said.

"Is that all you can say?" asked the genie. "How about thanks?"

"Yeah, thanks," Andrew said. "Thanks a lot!" he added.

"Anything else?"

"Well . . ." Just then he heard his sister's voice. "That's Susie," he told the genie. "She's only six, but she's okay, usually. Except for one thing. She's already almost as tall as me."

Jo leaned over and blinked twice, measuring Andrew with his eyes. "Hmmm," he said.

"Yeah," said Andrew. "I need those inches! But listen—she's been wishing and wishing for a watch. Could you blow up one for her?"

"Gold or silver?"

"Gold, I guess. No—wait. Could you make it purple?" It occurred to Andrew that he could explain a purple watch quicker than a gold one, if he had to.

"No problem!" said the genie. He blew at Andrew's hand, and there in his palm lay a purple watch.

Andrew checked the time. Exactly the same as the alarm clock by his bed. Two forty-five on Sunday afternoon.

"Thanks," he said. "You do great magic, Jo."

"I do, that's true. But there is a small peculiarity about my magic, Andrew—"

But Andrew wasn't listening. "Uncle Donald isn't going to like losing you, Jo. He'll be mad, you know?"

"Maybe, but it was his own fault. He was careless. And he knows the way my magic—"

"A bike!" Andrew interrupted again. "Can you blow me up a bike?"

"One of my best things!" Jo bounced up and down. "Any particular color?"

"I always wanted a silver bike. Could you make it silver? Put it around the side of the house, though. I don't want to explain it today." He grinned. "I don't see how I could."

"No problem!" The genie puckered up again. When Andrew looked sideways out the window, he saw the end of a silver fender and a taillight behind the bushes by the corner of the house.

"All right!" It was worth it! He'd figure out an explanation tomorrow. Somehow.

"Now, there is one thing. . . ." began the genie, but Andrew grabbed the bottle.

"That's my mom yelling. I have to go. Hop inside."

He opened the shoe-polish bottle.

The genie's toes uncurled. He looked suddenly smaller and terribly sad. "Don't you have a cleaner jar?"

Andrew glanced around. "Do you mind one that smells peanut-buttery?" he asked.

"Try me," said the genie.

The empty peanut-butter jar sat on top of the bookshelf with Andrew's collecting equipment. Andrew opened it, and the genie swirled inside, settled down on the bottom, and winked at him.

"Smells good," he said. "Now, listen—" but Andrew's mother called again. Andrew turned the cap tight and hid the bottle behind the butterfly net.

He met Susie in the hallway and gave her the purple watch.

"It's magic," he whispered. "When we go out with the folks today, hide it under your sleeve until I tell you. Don't show it off."

"Oh, Andrew!" was all she said, but her smile was thanks enough. She wasn't a bad kid.

"Remember—it's a secret." Until I figure out how to convince the folks I didn't steal it, he thought.

Andrew and Susie climbed into their family station

wagon. As Dad backed the car into the street, Andrew peered from the back window at the bushes near the corner of the house. He saw a silver line—one new bike, and all his!

He closed his eyes, the better to see the piles of green bills and gold coins filling his pockets. A TV for his room would be great. Another new bike would be nice, maybe red this time. And two skateboards—one for holidays! And—

Susie moved on the seat beside him. As he opened his left eye, she pulled her sleeve back and touched the purple watch.

"Secret!" he whispered, and reminded her, hard, with his elbow.

It was three o'clock on Sunday afternoon.

3

Peculiar Magic

At five minutes after three on Monday, Mrs. Carson grabbed Andrew by the collar.

"Don't wiggle, Andrew. You'll tear your shirt," she said, and pulled him out of line and back into Room Eight.

"Is something the matter, Mrs. Carson?"

"Something indeed." She picked the top paper from the pile of homework. His name was there in his own writing. The problems were there. But the answers were gone. "Is this a joke?" she asked.

Andrew swallowed so hard, he thought his voice was gone too.

"Someone erased them, Mrs. Carson." He bent his head way back to look up at her. "They were there, honest."

He knew that. He'd checked them with his calculator right after breakfast, just in case Jo had made a mistake.

Mrs. Carson glared down at Andrew. "When you finish tomorrow's assignment, do this one. And check each problem on another sheet, young man."

What she meant was that he had to copy each problem in reverse and work it again to see if his answers matched. That meant forty problems, each done twice—

"And one more thing. Tomorrow is the last possible day to give your book report. Do it or take an F. Goodbye, Andrew," said Mrs. Carson.

He turned around and bumped right into Kevin Clark.

"Guess you don't always do your homework," Kevin said, laughing at him. "You're just like the rest of us after all, aren't you?"

Andrew brushed past without answering. He wasn't like the rest of them. For one thing, he had a genie whose magic didn't work.

When he stepped out the side door of the school, the April wind hit him. So did his sister.

"It's gone!" With her hands on her hips, she looked ready to pop him again. "My watch disappeared, Andrew. I peeked just before the bell, and it was gone. Where is it, Andrew?"

"How do I know? I told you it was magic."

"But I love it and it's gone." She rubbed her eyes with

a clenched fist, and Andrew sidestepped around, out of reach. "Do something, Andrew!"

"I'll try. You go on home, Susie. I have to get my bike!"

He ran, but he wasn't too surprised when he reached the bike rack out in front of the school and found that the only thing left was his old bike lock, still closed.

After all the trouble he'd taken! He'd made sure Mom had gone to work and Dad was safely in his office at the back of the house and Susie had started off before he'd wheeled the silver bike out of hiding.

The perfect bicycle! Ten speeds and a streak of red through the silver, the very bike Andrew had seen once and gone crazy over.

It was nearly three thirty when he crashed breathlessly into his own house, stuck his head in his father's office to yell, "I'm home!" and raced upstairs.

He slammed his bedroom door and grabbed the peanut-butter jar. It looked empty except for a streak of brown he must have missed when he washed it out.

Andrew opened the jar and Jo appeared, balancing on the rim.

"Good," he said. "You're home."

"Listen, what sort of a genie are you? You got me into

a lot of trouble, you know that?" Andrew shook the jar. "I'll be working until midnight, and it's all your fault."

The genie landed on the dictionary and reached over to curl his toes. "Something wrong?"

"Wrong! Your magic disappears, you know that?"

"Of course I know that. I tried to tell you yesterday, but you wouldn't listen. I'm a twenty-four-hour genie," he said. "My magic lasts exactly twenty-four hours. No more, no less."

"No more, no less," repeated Andrew, and he flopped on the bed, holding his head while visions of gold coins and skateboards streamed out of it and disappeared.

Jo began a set of jumping jacks. His curls danced up and down, and his blue toes flashed and sparkled. When he reached ten, he stopped and shook himself and said he felt better.

"Now brighten up," he told Andrew. "My magic may be short, but it's splendid. You'll see."

"It's rotten."

"It most certainly is not."

"It's useless!"

"It isn't that, either. Just sit up and think."

Andrew sat up and thought.

"Well, one thing," he said after a moment. "If you make a mistake, it fixes itself in a day."

"Genies do not make mistakes," said Jo.

"Not often, anyhow," muttered Andrew. "Can you at least give Susie back her purple watch? For a day?"

"Would red do?"

"She likes purple."

"But, Andrew, I can't make the same magic twice. It's a rule."

Never the same thing twice? That meant no more silver bikes, even for a day. Andrew said that was crazy.

"Crazy? Just a little peculiar, Andrew. Besides, a person who hangs stuffed bats in his room should not call other people crazy."

Andrew rolled over and looked at the brown bat flying above his head. He glanced at the bat poster on the wall.

"Aren't they great? Uncle Donald brought them last year."

"I'm not surprised," sniffed Jo. "Now then, what next?"

The safest and most sensible answer to that was to pack Jo away, thought Andrew. Not the easiest answer, but the most sensible. He reached for the shoe-polish bottle.

"Just hop in," he said in a stern voice. "Hop. Right now."

"That is not friendly!" The genie backed up against the book bag. His toes were straight, his cheeks pale.

"You have to give me a chance, Andrew. You'll see. I can help you a lot."

Andrew placed the black polish bottle on the left side of his lamp. He placed the peanut-butter jar on the right side. He folded his arms and frowned at the genie.

"Okay," he said. "Make me two inches taller."

4

Excellent Magic!

"No," said Jo.

The genie climbed on top of the brown book bag and sat down. He crossed his legs and pulled his toes up and curled the blue ends. He tugged at one black curl. "Let's talk about what *else* you want," he said.

"Two inches," said Andrew.

"Use your imagination, my friend. That is too much length to add overnight."

"But just for a while. Please Jo?"

"Just for a while? Impossible. It would be a disaster, I promise you." The genie rocked back and forth, his arms folded across his chest. The matter seemed closed. "What else did you say you wanted?"

Andrew glared; you can't hit someone only six inches tall, but he sure wanted to. All he asked was to be two inches taller for a little while. He wasn't asking for the moon.

"If I promise not to go out of this room?"

The small genie looked earnestly at Andrew. "Please don't ask," he said. "You wouldn't like it at all."

"Okay, okay, okay! What else, then?"

"That's my question," Jo said happily. "What do you want or need or hope for?"

Andrew thought, and then he poked the blue genie very gently on the shoulder.

"Can you give book reports?" he asked.

"You haven't read the book yet, right?" asked Jo.

"Of course I've read it. What do you think I am?"

Jo blinked. "Just kidding," he said.

"You'd better be. I know my report by heart. I'm all ready to give it. I even have what Mrs. Carson calls visual aids, stuff to show. It's a good report."

"Then what's the problem?"

"Oh, well—you know—" Andrew flicked some dirt from his shoes.

The genie cocked his head. "Stage fright?"

"More like scared to death! Whenever I stand up and everyone looks at me, my knees wobble and my throat gets stiff—" Andrew took off his glasses and wiped his forehead with his sleeve. "Just thinking about it makes me sweat."

"But you've done reports before, haven't you?"

"Not until this year. Mrs. Carson doesn't take any

excuse. The first time . . ." Andrew hid his face.

"You survived," said Jo cheerily. "You're still here."

"I wet my pants," whispered Andrew.

"Ouch," said Jo.

"Yeah. And in January, I got sick and had to run for the restroom."

"Really sick?"

"Yucky sick. So now—she says if I put it off one more day, I flunk."

"Meaning?"

"Fail. Get an F for the whole grading period. My dad will kill me, and Mom will help him."

The genie leaped to his feet. "Now brighten up there, Andrew, and get ready!"

"For what, exactly?" Andrew clamped his glasses on and backed away.

Six inches of excited genie jumped from the book bag and ran to the edge of the desk.

"Come back here! I am about to make you the best public speaker in the whole wide world!"

"The best in Room Eight will do," Andrew said. "Are you sure it will last for twenty-four hours?"

"Didn't I say so? Now—" Jo leaned toward Andrew. *"No problem!"* he shouted, and blew.

"Wonderful magic," he said as he sat down again. "Magnificent magic," he added as he crossed his legs.

Andrew sat too. He actually felt different already—braver, more confident, taller. . . .

Taller? He leaped toward the mirror; no such luck. He wasn't any taller.

At suppertime Susie pulled Andrew into the hallway downstairs.

"Look!" Lifting the pink cuff of her shirt, she showed him a narrow green watch.

"Well, well," Andrew started. Then he grinned. "Like it?"

"I love it! But you know what?" She dropped the cuff and whispered in his ear. "We'd better keep it a secret!"

"Right," said Andrew. "Don't get too crazy about it either. Tomorrow it might be red, or have Roman numerals."

Later, as soon as the dishes were cleared, Andrew said he had homework to do, which was true, and raced upstairs.

He dropped the peanut-butter jar in his haste; an unhappy genie blew itself into shape a moment later.

"Is that any way to wake a person?" Jo asked, curling his left toe.

"Sorry. Now listen—I saw Susie's watch, Jo. You blew me into a good speaker. I feel different already."

"'Of course," said Jo, blowing gently at his puffy blue sleeve.

"Stop that and listen! If your magic is that good, make me two inches taller!"

Jo blew at his other sleeve before he answered.

"I told you that wouldn't work," he said. "You'd be mad as a wet peacock if I did that."

"Please, Jo? Just this once?"

"I cannot do it," the genie said with a little sigh.

"You mean you won't do it. Okay, forget this friendly stuff," Andrew stood as tall as he could and spoke loud and clear. "I'm the master, and I say make me two inches taller."

"Ah, Master," Jo said, bowing and curling the other toe while he was down there. "Why not three inches?"

"Good. Make it three inches."

"No."

"Choose where you live then," Andrew said. He held one bottle in each hand. "Make me taller, and you can smell peanut butter. Refuse, and you go back in the closet."

"I have a fool for a master!" Jo raised up on tiptoes and shook his fists. "There! *No problem!*" He blew hard at Andrew. "Don't blame me if you hate it."

Jo disappeared with a swirl of blue into the peanut-butter jar, and Andrew leaped toward the mirror.

He was three inches taller, and it was twenty after seven on Monday night.

5

No More, No Less

Andrew looked down. His feet were definitely farther away.

He saw the book he'd lost two days ago on top of the chest of drawers.

He looked eye to eye with the brown bat in the poster and almost eye to eye with the stuffed one flying over his bed.

Andrew patted the bat's head.

On tiptoes he could just touch the tip of the red bat hanging upside down in the corner.

He easily reached back on the closet shelf and grabbed his baseball glove—the one he hadn't used yet. His father had given it to him for Christmas, as if he thought Andrew might want it come spring.

Spring had come, and Andrew still didn't want it. He and David had always been too busy for sports. Besides, anyone as short as he *usually* was didn't have a chance playing with Kevin and those guys. He could stand right out in the open and they'd never pick him for a team. Andrew knew that for sure.

He tossed the glove back onto the shelf.

Bending over, he touched his toes, and had to stretch some to do that. His glasses slid down his nose, and his pants slid down on his hips.

I'm skinnier, he thought, and pulled in his belt.

"Andrew?" Susie banged on the door and opened it. "Andrew? Listen—" She stopped. "What's wrong with you?"

"Can't you ever wait after you knock? Who asked you—" He stopped. "What are you talking about?"

"Your pants! Where did you get those pants?" Her hands flew to cover her mouth, but it was no help; she laughed so hard, she had to lean against the door.

"What about my pants?"

"They're short!"

"They are?" Andrew looked down. They were. Really short!

"Mom will flip," she said. "I don't understand. *Oh.*" Slowly she looked up, until their eyes met. "Andrew, you grew. Is it more magic?"

"Of course it's magic, but don't worry—it won't last long. I just wanted to see how it felt."

"Do you like it?"

"Sure I do. A lot."

"Good. But you better be regular size by morning or Mom will die."

"Don't be stupid, Susie. I'll be fine. Just don't tell." He was tempted to introduce her to Jo, but he didn't. "Magic—and a secret," he said instead.

"Okay, but I wouldn't come downstairs that way if I were you," she warned.

Andrew did his math, finishing faster than ever before. Because I'm taller, he thought, and laughed at himself. Then he touched everything that was normally out of his reach, tried once more to touch the red bat with the foxlike face hanging in the corner, and finally gave the peanut-butter jar a shake.

"Jo? Come out and make me the right size again, will you? I have to go downstairs."

"I can't," Jo said from deep in the jar.

"What?"

"I can't. Twenty-four hours. No more, no less. Remember?"

Andrew froze. His only working part was his heart, and that was slowly sliding toward his stomach.

"But, Jo. 'No more, no less'—that's just something people say. They don't mean it." He sank onto the desk chair. "Like Susie said Mom would die. She didn't mean that would really happen. It's a figure of speech, Jo."

Jo's face appeared over the edge of the jar, and his dark eyes flashed at Andrew.

"Not a figure of speech, Andrew, but the plain and simple fact. My magic lasts twenty-four hours. No more, no less."

"But, Jo, look at me! I have to go to school tomorrow."

"You will change back when the time is up. Even if I wanted to, which I do not, I cannot change your command."

Andrew pressed both hands flat against his desk, hearing the sound of his own voice in his head. *I'm the master,* he'd said.

"I'm sorry, Jo," he said, and he really was. "Honestly, I didn't mean that master stuff. Don't be mad. Can we be friends again? Please?"

Jo's dark eyes stared soberly at Andrew. "Until the next time?" he asked.

"Never. I'll never say it again," Andrew declared.

"Good," Jo said. "Friends again, then, but I still can't change you."

Andrew lifted an arm, and his shirt cuff pulled back; it was three inches too short.

"Roll up your sleeves," Jo said.

Andrew called downstairs to tell his family he was going to bed. Of course his mother came up to see if he felt all right, but by then he was safely under the covers, with his knees bent.

"I'm fine," he said. "I just thought I might be sick in the morning, you know, so I figured to get a little extra sleep."

His mother was not born last week. "Do you have to give your book report?" she asked, and he nodded.

"But that's okay," he assured her. "I'll give a great report. No problem," he added, grinning, and returned her hug.

In the morning he did feel sick, but only about the length of his pants. His ankles looked silly sticking out so far.

He opened the peanut-butter jar.

"Jo, please wake up! Please give me some pants that fit."

Jo opened one eye. *"No problem!"* he said sleepily, and blew at Andrew.

"Thanks! Whoops—hey! What do you call these?" His jeans had turned into scarlet silk trousers all bunched at the ankles.

"I call them beautiful," Jo said.

Andrew wriggled out of the silk as fast as he could wriggle. "Just ordinary jeans will do, Jo. Hurry, or I'll be late to school."

"I can't. Sorry," Jo answered.

Andrew's heart dropped again as he bent over to pick up the trousers. Those words sounded too familiar.

"Explain," he said, although he didn't want to hear it.

"It's simple," Jo said. "My magic lasts twenty-four hours."

"No matter what," Andrew put in.

"Yes. And I cannot do exactly the same thing twice, ever."

"But blue jeans are not the same as these things!" Andrew tossed the red silk toward the bed. "Besides, you made Susie another watch, a green one."

"Ah, but that was twenty-four hours after the first watch, and it was not exactly alike. You see?"

The genie climbed onto the edge of the jar, looking earnestly at Andrew.

"I could make you a blue bike now," he said. "One each twenty-four hours. But never two alike."

Andrew dumped Jo into the jar, rear-end first.

"See you tonight," he said, and closed the lid.

He found an old pair of jeans. They were as tight and short as his regular pair.

He pulled up his socks. That helped a little.

He pushed up his sweater sleeves. That helped too.

Sliding into the kitchen, he sat on his chair before his mother had a look at him. She was on her way out the door anyhow, and didn't look too hard.

"All set for today?" she asked.

Andrew said, "You bet," and drank his juice. He chewed his cereal in double time, all the while wondering if the kids at school would notice his pants. They would, of course. And the snobs, like Kevin Clark, would laugh at him.

But he had to go. He was almost out the door with his book and the bag of stuff for his report before his father lifted his eyes from the paper. "Good luck," he said.

"Thanks," said Andrew.

Then his father lifted himself, too.

"Those pants from last year? What's the idea?"

"New style," Andrew said, and made it out the door. Outside, he stopped and turned up the bottom of each pant leg. If you must look silly, he told himself, you might as well look as though you mean it.

6

Walking Tall

Andrew avoided walking close to anyone on the way into school. His friend David would have laughed if he had found himself in the same fix, but he wasn't David—he was Andrew, and scared stiff that someone would notice how tall he was all of a sudden!

As soon as he thought David's name, he wished he hadn't. It made him cross to remember the fun they used to have. It reminded him that he was lonely.

Inside, he flopped into his seat and slid down a little. Dawn Brown, at the desk behind him, would notice fast as anything if he stuck up farther than he ought to.

He stayed scrunched down and quiet, thanking his lucky stars that this wasn't gym day. When the class lined up in the hall to go to the rest rooms, Andrew curved his head into a book and said he didn't have to. Mrs. Carson came back and stood beside him.

"Andrew?" she said. He slid out on the far side of his

desk and tried to look short as he walked alone up the aisle.

Kevin was last in line, like always. Billy Moss was right in front of him.

Andrew hung back, hoping Kevin wouldn't notice they could look eyeball to eyeball *without* Andrew standing on tiptoes.

Kevin and Billy stared at his rolled-up pants.

"How come?" Billy pointed.

Andrew hunched his head into his shoulders and grinned, cheerfully, he hoped. "I like them that way," he said.

Back at his desk, Andrew's shoulders ached from slouching. He breathed slowly in and out, trying to remember all he'd ever read about staying calm. It wasn't much, and it didn't help.

It was a long morning.

When the classroom clock said eleven thirty, Mrs. Carson still hadn't called on him.

If she forgot, he wouldn't have to stand up in front of everyone in rolled-up pants. But if he had to wait for tomorrow, Jo's magic would be gone. He would never be the best speaker in Room Eight.

He wiggled in his seat and cleaned his glasses and cleared his throat, and suddenly she looked at the clock.

"Clear your desks and fold your hands, class. Andrew

is ready to give his book report," she announced. "Finally," she added.

Twenty-nine faces looked at him. Andrew waited for his stomach to turn inside out. It didn't.

He stood up, and his knees held firm.

He marched to the front of the room and turned around and looked back at the twenty-nine faces. He opened his mouth, and then he swallowed, hard. Was he going to be sick again?

"First of all," he said, and when his voice came out normally, he relaxed a little. Good magic! "This book won a couple of prizes. But don't pay any attention to that. It's still about the best book I ever read."

Everyone laughed, even Mrs. Carson, and Andrew waited for the laughter to stop or himself to faint, whichever came first. When the quiet came, he went on without a tremble.

"If I ran away to live off the land, my mom would call the cops. And then the Marines. Wouldn't yours?" He waited a second and lots of kids nodded their heads. They were listening!

"Well, in this book, Sam goes off like that, and his folks let him."

When he told about Sam trying to make a fire the first night he spent all alone in the mountain woods, he brought out a piece of flint and a steel file.

"This is what Sam used. I've been practicing, and it's still hard to do," he said. He held up a small bag of tinder and looked at the teacher.

"No demonstrations, Andrew," she said, and the class groaned.

At the part about Sam finding something to put his food in, he brought out the turtle shell he'd carried from home.

"This is what Sam used for a bowl, and it works real well. I tried it," said Andrew.

He sat down a few moments later, and the class clapped for a long time; of course, they clapped for any dumb thing, but this time he knew they liked it, and he was not sick or damp or dead or anything!

Except starving, but it was time for lunch.

After school he couldn't go right home because the kids surrounded him, out in the school yard.

"Make a fire," they insisted. The wind was blocked by at least half of his class, so the tinder caught right away.

"Let me try it!"

Everyone wanted a turn. Andrew figured he wouldn't have enough tinder, but he was wrong. The tinder lasted because hardly anyone could do it.

"You have to practice," he told them.

"Like baseball," Kevin said. "Come on, we're going to practice today, right here. Sign-up is next week!"

Andrew couldn't believe it. Kevin was looking right at him and talking about Little League as if he, Andrew, would be playing. As if he was expected, as if he might even be a regular on a team!

"We'll meet back here in fifteen minutes," Kevin said, and raced behind Billy across the school yard. Andrew gathered his belongings and raced too—for home, and for his bedroom.

"Please, Jo, please do it," he begged while he scrambled out of his school shirt and into an old sweatshirt, pushing the sleeves high on his arms. "Aren't we friends again?"

"No more magic until I hear about the book report," the genie said.

"An A!" Andrew's hand met Jo's in a low high-five. "I'll tell you all about it tonight. I promise. Just for now, make me a decent ballplayer. I can't go unless you do. Not perfect, just decent—okay?"

"Why not perfect?" asked Jo. He stood with arms akimbo, head cocked toward Andrew. "Perfect is nice."

"Perfect is unreal," Andrew said. He looked up from tying his second sneaker. "Save perfect."

He stood up and stretched as tall as he could go. It was a lot farther than he'd ever stretched before.

"No one will notice how tall I am on the field, and I haven't ever in my life before been asked to play ball."

"Ah," said Jo. "Do you like to play?"

"No, not especially." Andrew grinned. "But that's not the point. I'd like to play with the guys, just to see if I might like it."

"Can I go along?"

"No way. You might get squashed when I slide. *If* I slide," he added with an explosion of laughter.

"Genies don't squash," Jo said indignantly.

"All the same, you better not."

He grabbed his glove from high on the shelf and crushed it in his hands, then pounded it with his fist.

"Please, Jo, blow me into a ballplayer. Fair to good."

"But not perfect. *No problem!*" said Jo, and he blew his magic air at Andrew.

7

Who's Stuck Up?

By suppertime, when the teams fell apart because the players were hungry, Andrew felt wonderful and tired and definitely confused. There was something he needed to ask Jo.

He'd dropped a few balls out in right field, and he'd missed a few pitches. *But* he had made three hits, one of them almost a home run, and he'd thrown Billy out at first with a throw so long he couldn't believe it.

All the guys yelled when he did it.

"Way to go!" they'd hollered.

That was the best feeling he could remember. But even so, something strange was going on.

"That was some good pass I made, wasn't it?" he said to Kevin as they started home.

Kevin stopped wiping his face and stared at Andrew over the sleeve of his orange sweatshirt. "A good what?" he asked.

"A pass. A good— Oh, wrong game. Sorry!" Andrew's

face got hot, and he dropped his glove. Smooth as silk, his foot came up and kicked that mitt high in the air, across the school yard, and out to the center of the street.

A dark-blue Honda ran over it.

"You're nuts!" shouted Kevin. He took off, running for the glove.

Andrew ran too, but he felt much better. He'd been dying to kick something for an hour and a half!

Kevin reached the glove first, brushed it off, and handed it to Andrew without a word.

Andrew patted the mitt and pushed his hand into it. "Just breaking it in," he said. Then he finally looked Kevin in the eye, and after a moment they both started laughing.

"Want to be on my side tomorrow? For baseball?" asked Kevin. And then they laughed some more.

At the corner nearest Andrew's house, Kevin turned in the other direction.

"You aren't as stuck up as I thought," he said, stepping down to the street. Then he stopped and pointed. "Either we played late or that one woke up early."

Puzzled, Andrew looked at the sky. One lone bat circled, darted for a mouthful of bugs, and then circled again. Kevin is not the sort to notice bats, he thought. He's just a jock, isn't he?

But if not the bat, then what was he talking about?

It must have been the bat.

The clock said nineteen minutes after seven when he opened the jar that night. As Jo pulled and blew his curly toes into shape, Andrew felt a jerk, and he was three inches shorter, just that quick.

"And that's that," he said.

"Well, were you a good ballplayer?" Jo asked as he began a set of jumping jacks. "Were. You. Won. Der. Ful?"

"Good enough," said Andrew. "Just the way I wanted, actually. But listen, Jo, have you ever seen a ballgame?"

"Seen. One? Cer. Tain. Ly!" Hands on hips, Jo stopped jumping and leaned his face toward Andrew's. "Why do you ask?"

"I just wondered, is all. I played pretty good, but I had to work at it all the time. It seemed as if I—"

"Good," interrupted Jo. "You needn't expect me to do everything. Do you play tomorrow?"

"Without magic? That'd be suicide. They'd see how I really play, and that would do it. They're the most stuck-up—"

Andrew's chin hit the back of the chair. His teeth clicked as they met. He'd just remembered something. Just heard it, actually, in his head.

"What's the trouble?" Jo danced to the edge of the desk and jumped to the back of Andrew's hand.

Andrew's mouth opened and shut again. Slowly he turned his hand so that Jo could clamber over and sit in his palm.

"Look at me," he demanded, frowning. "Do I look friendly, open, kind, considerate, helpful—"

"No," Jo said.

"Oh. Well, I am. And Kevin said I wasn't as stuck-up as he thought! He's got nerve, calling me stuck-up! Can you believe that?"

"Of course," said Jo.

Andrew closed his fingers but Jo slid up and out and landed gracefully on the desk, turning a bright shade of yellow.

"Genies do not squish," he told Andrew, and leaned over to pull and curl the ends of his yellow shoes. "Now tell me something. 'Stuck-up' means pretty pleased with yourself, right? Conceited?"

"Yes, but I'm not. I'm not like that at all, Jo."

"Then why don't you play ball with the guys? You don't have to wait to be asked, I think."

"But I'm not any good. Honest." Andrew stood up and pushed his hands deep into his pockets. "You just don't know how they laugh at kids who aren't any good."

"The same way they laugh at genies who can make only twenty-four-hour magic, I suppose."

Andrew turned quickly. "Do they?"

"Of course they do. Want a candy bar?"

"Yes, please."

Jo said, *"No problem!"* and a chocolate bar appeared on the desk. As Andrew unwrapped it, a funny thought struck. "I'll never get fat eating your magic candy, will I?"

"Not a chance. It disappears in twenty-four hours. How do you know this Kevin wouldn't like other things you like, as well as baseball?"

"I just know, that's all."

"Now that sounds conceited to me!" Jo jumped onto the dictionary and sat down, looking pleased with himself.

"I'm not conceited," Andrew said.

Jo cocked his head and raised his eyebrows and stared at the ceiling. Andrew decided to go downstairs.

"Don't worry," Jo said. "Tomorrow at school we'll see who is the stuck-up one."

"It's not me!" Andrew reached for the peanut-butter jar and stopped still. "Who's 'we'? You can't go to school!"

"Certainly I can. How can I help if I don't see these friends of yours?"

"I don't need any help, I am not conceited, and they are not my friends."

"Then they ought to be, don't you think?"

"No, I do not think that." Andrew opened the jar and Jo blew at him, blew into the air, and swirled inside.

"No problem! No problem!" he cried.

"Hah. I'll see you tomorrow, after school." As Andrew closed the lid, he heard Jo laughing through the glass.

On the way downstairs he met Susie racing up.

"Look! It was just all of a sudden on my arm. It's peach colored, Andrew. Isn't it amazing?"

"Spectacular." So that's why Jo blew into the air, he thought. And I bet I know why he blew at me!

8

Genies Do Not Squish

Andrew was right. Jo had magicked him into opening his jar in the morning, whether he wanted to or not.

"I'll ride in your pocket," Jo said as soon as he was free. "Genies do not bulge."

By the time Andrew slid his legs under the desk at school, he knew Jo was right. No one could guess he had a genie on board—yet.

"Who's that?" Jo whispered in his ear. Andrew's hand smacked his head to hide Jo, but all he felt was air and sting.

"Who's that?" Jo repeated.

"Mrs. Carson, of course. The teacher."

"She's really tall," Jo said.

Mary Lou, in front of Andrew, turned around. "I don't know what you said, but shut up anyhow."

"Sorry," Andrew said.

Later, Jo whispered again. "Which one is Kevin?"

"Blue shirt," Andrew whispered back. Mary Lou's shoulders twitched in front of him.

"He looks okay."

"He is. I mean, he's stuck-up, like I said, but he's okay, too. He pitches good."

Mary Lou turned all the way around and squinched her eyes at Andrew.

"I know, shut up anyway," he whispered.

"You'd better. Who's stuck-up?" she asked.

"You." He yanked his book up to avoid her swishing hand and was glad she hadn't screamed. Screaming was her favorite thing.

Mrs. Carson closed her book.

"Time for recess, class, and when we come back, I want you to go to the office, Andrew."

"What'd I do?"

"Nothing that I know of. There are papers to collate, and I promised to send someone to help. Can you manage that?"

"If someone tells me what it means, I can," he said.

Out in the school yard, Andrew ambled over to the wall and leaned against it.

"Get up front! How will you get picked back here?" Jo's voice buzzed like an irritated bug in his ear.

"I always stand back here."

"No wonder you get picked last. Get up front!"

Andrew shoved his back against the wall, determined not to move, but then—*pow!* He was right up in front, and he didn't even know how he got there. He hated Red Rover. He had always hated it. Racing across the field and trying to break through the enemy line was disgusting. He would not do it. But then—

"Andrew, come on my side," Kevin called finally, and Jo shoved Andrew into the line.

A moment later Billy yelled from across the way. "Red Rover, Red Rover, let Andrew come over!"

With a sigh Andrew ran across the open space—and *burst* through their line! He couldn't believe it. He grabbed Dawn and pulled her back to his own side.

Jo must have done it. Andrew had never broken through a line before that he could remember, which was why he'd always hated this game.

"Thanks," he said out loud to no one in particular, hoping Jo would hear. Then he shouted for Billy to come over.

Billy charged across the open space, heading for Andrew and Dawn. Seconds later he was flat on his back.

"Hey, you were supposed to break hands!" He scrambled to his feet. "How come you didn't?"

"I don't know," Dawn said, giggling. "Come on, you can stand here."

Billy dusted his pants. "But you always break," he muttered to Andrew before taking his place on their side.

No one could break through Andrew's line. Soon it was twice as long as the other one.

"No fun," Kevin complained, and he was right. It wasn't much fun when no one could break through no matter what. Andrew knew he must explain that to Jo when he had a chance.

Luckily Mrs. Carson stopped the game, and they marched inside. Andrew went straight to the principal's office. The secretary took him to the next room and showed him how to walk around the table, picking up eight sheets in order and stapling them at the corner. Then she went out, closing the door behind her.

"Jo? You here?" asked Andrew.

"Of course I'm here!" Jo appeared in the center of the table. "Someone's coming!" Then he disappeared.

Kevin stepped inside. "So show me," he said. "She figured you'd need help."

"It's really tough." Andrew grinned. "You even have to walk around the table." He showed Kevin how to pick up the sheets and staple them.

"I see what you mean." Kevin wiped his hands on his jeans and picked up the first sheet.

Andrew, following behind, wondered what they could talk about. Except for baseball, he didn't know what Kevin liked.

Jo would say he ought to find out, but how he was to do that?

"Just ask!" exploded Jo in Andrew's ear, and Andrew laughed out loud. Trust Jo to read his mind.

"What's so funny?"

"Us, going around in circles."

"Better than art class, anyhow."

"I don't mind art," Andrew said, and Kevin smacked his papers on the table.

"You wouldn't. You're good at everything, aren't you? You don't mind spelling, either."

"Neither do you," Andrew said, and Kevin hit the stapler.

"Spelling's my worst subject. Must be nice to be good at everything."

"Good! You must be crazy." Andrew picked up two pink sheets by mistake and put one back. "I'm awful at games, and I'm scared to stand up in front of the class. You call that good? Everyone can do that except me."

Kevin slammed the stapler again. "Yesterday you weren't scared. You ever hear anything from David, that kid you were friends with?"

"Not much," said Andrew. "He likes it in Hartford, I guess."

"Good. He didn't like anything here, for sure. Except you. What are you doing for the science fair next year?"

"Next year?" Andrew blinked. "How do I know?"

"Well, you did bats last time, and I just wondered."

Andrew took off his glasses to wipe them. "You decided what you're doing?" he asked.

"This soon? You're crazy." Kevin looked at the yellow sheet as if he were reading it. Then, without looking up, he said, "I thought insects, maybe. Something about them. Those ugly tomato ones, maybe."

"Yuck. You'll have to start collecting this summer—"

Loud screams from somewhere!

"What's that?" Andrew said.

Kevin yanked the door open. "From our end of the hall, and not just Mary Lou! Come on!"

They passed the principal racing down the hall.

9

No One Saw That

"Hey!" yelled Kevin.

"Hey!" yelled Andrew, right behind him. "What's wrong?"

The screams stopped. Everyone in Room Eight was crouched in the aisles with their hands on their heads, except for Mrs. Carson, who was crouched on the floor beside her desk.

"Get down!"

"Why?"

"A bat!"

The principal, behind Andrew, crouched immediately. "Where?" she asked.

Kevin and Andrew stepped inside, and a bat swooped down the center of the room, circled at the end, and swooped back. Both boys flattened themselves against the wall.

"I'll get Mr. Hyde," the principal called, and she disappeared, pushing the door shut behind her.

"He'll kill it," Andrew said. "He'd better not kill it, Mrs. Carson."

"He'd better not," Kevin added. "More people die from Sunday-school picnics than from bats. Honestly, Mrs. Carson."

Prickles marched up the back of Andrew's head. That was right out of his own science report. He couldn't believe Kevin remembered that.

Mrs. Carson's foot slipped; she sat flat on the floor. "This is not a picnic," she said.

The bat swooped again as if to prove it. Mary Lou screamed.

"We have to do something. Right now," Kevin said.

"Like what?" asked Andrew.

"Open the window," Jo said.

Kevin's head snapped toward Andrew. "Open the window? He'll never go out—too much sunshine."

"Maybe he will." Andrew sidled along the wall. Kevin followed.

"You boys get down," Mrs. Carson said, and Andrew waved his hand a little, reassuring her.

"Just going to give him someplace to go," he said.

"Except he won't." But Kevin followed Andrew, and when they reached the window wall, he helped push.

"Stuck," muttered Andrew.

"No problem," whispered Jo, and *whoosh*, the window

went up to the top. Andrew looked up and hoped it wouldn't rain before tomorrow this time.

"Now what?" Kevin asked, and Andrew shook his head.

"I wish I knew."

The bat swooped again, and three boys in Billy's row flopped flat on the floor, laughing. At least, Andrew thought they were laughing. He wasn't sure.

"Too close!" cried one.

"I'm fainting!" screamed Mary Lou, and Dawn grabbed at her.

"Don't you dare!"

Mr. Hyde, the custodian, stuck his head in the door, then stepped inside with a broom in his hand.

"Knew this would happen," he announced cheerfully. "That Room Six always has to keep her window open at the top. I told her a dozen times she'd forget to close it one day, and —"

"Never mind how it got here, Mr. Hyde. Just get it out. Alive, if possible," Mrs. Carson said, glancing at Kevin and Andrew.

"Alive? Not likely. I'll get him though—don't worry." Then the bat flew again and Mr. Hyde ducked, right out of the room.

"Next time," he said, slipping inside again, keeping

his back flat against the door. "You kids stay down there."

Andrew didn't think anyone was about to stand up at the moment. He didn't think Mr. Hyde ought to use his broom, either.

"We could get a butterfly net," he said, and Kevin said, "Great, but where?"

"By your coat," Jo whispered.

"By my coat," Andrew said.

Head up but eyes on the bat, he sidled along the wall to the coatracks, felt behind his windbreaker, and took out a long-handled net.

Mrs. Carson didn't ask how it got there. "What will you do with that?" she asked instead.

"Like this—" The bat flew, and Andrew swung the net. He missed.

The bat flew again. Andrew missed again.

Kevin grabbed the handle, swung the net, and missed.

Mr. Hyde moved closer with his broom. "I'll try it, boys," he said.

He missed too. The bat swooshed safely by. Andrew and Kevin grinned at each other.

Suddenly, from the back of the room, Jo's voice shouted, "SHUT YOUR EYES! TIGHT! NOW! SHUT YOUR EYES!"

Andrew whirled and saw a wide, dark cloud spread like a path from the bat to the open window. Seconds later the bat glided down the path and disappeared. The cloud rolled up and disappeared too.

"I did not see that," said Mrs. Carson, and then she closed her eyes.

Everyone talked at once, and those who had seen the path told the ones who hadn't, but no one seemed to believe it had really happened.

Kevin and Andrew watched the dark cloud move up and out of sight beyond the school buildings.

"Whatever that was, it was better than a broom," Kevin said.

They stretched to pull the window down; it did not budge. Mr. Hyde came to help.

"Wish I hadn't closed my eyes," he said.

Between the three of them they could not get the window down.

"Sorry," whispered Jo in Andrew's ear.

"Why don't we leave it until tomorrow? It might get tired of sticking and come down by itself," said Andrew.

"Nonsense. We can't do that—" Mr. Hyde peered out, as though wondering how many thieves would crawl up the wall and into the room overnight. Or how many bats. He gave the window one more tug and said he would leave it for now, at least.

"You folks have your work to do," he said.

"Twenty-four hours will do it," Andrew said. "You'll see."

"Twenty-four hours will certainly do it." A new voice spoke from the open doorway.

"Oh, no," said Andrew.

"Oh, yes," said Uncle Donald.

10

Genies Do Not Escape

Andrew wasn't really surprised to see his uncle—he always turned up in unexpected places. And by now he would have missed his genie.

"That was a quick trip to the Arctic," Andrew said after the door clicked shut and they were alone in the hall.

"Wasn't it! Actually, I was only halfway there when I realized I was missing something. Have you had a good time these three days, Nephew?"

Andrew looked his uncle in the eye. "It was pretty interesting," he said. "Does Mom know you came back?"

"No, and your father doesn't either. Nor my good friend Susie. I used my key, I went up to your room, and I found this." He held the polish bottle upside down. "Empty."

"Oh," said Andrew.

"And this, beside it," added his uncle. He held the peanut-butter jar upside down too.

"That one smells better," Andrew explained.

"I don't doubt it. The polish bottle looks more normal in my luggage, however."

He raised his eyebrows at Andrew and added, "Where is our friend Jo?"

Andrew studied his shoes. Then he studied his uncle's shoes.

"How come you didn't have Jo magic you to the Arctic?"

"Think about it, Andrew."

Andrew thought, and then he grinned. "You'd end up right back here in twenty-four hours, right?"

"Right. Not long enough for all I hope to do there."

A third-grade class passed by in a line, on their way to the lunchroom. Uncle Donald put a bottle in each pocket of his jacket and dropped an arm across Andrew's shoulders. They walked toward the end of the hall.

"Where did you say Jo was?" he asked.

"I think he escaped," Andrew said. "We opened the window, and he rescued a bat—"

"Genies do not escape," Jo said out loud, and Uncle Donald laughed.

"He's right—they don't. Ready to travel, Jo?"

They stopped at the window and Jo appeared, dancing, on the wide sill. One long leap and he whirled, arms wide.

"Welcome," he began, but Andrew interrupted.

"I need you! Do I have to let you go? Is it a rule or something?"

Jo sat down.

"Not a rule, except the one about fair play," said Uncle Donald. "A matter of honor, don't you think? You found him in my box."

"The bottle fell out."

"All by itself?"

Andrew ignored that question and looked down at Jo.

"What about Susie? She likes having a different watch every day. She'll cry, I'll bet. And she never even met you, Jo!"

"Good." Uncle Donald smiled.

"And Kevin and me are just getting to be friends, a little, maybe. I need your help."

"Think so?" Jo looked at Uncle Donald with twinkling eyes. "I was a big help. When he wanted to be a good ballplayer, he meant baseball, but I made him into a football player."

Uncle Donald laughed, but Andrew's mouth dropped open.

"You did that on purpose, Jo? You knew you did that? I thought—"

"I was still a little mad at you, I think," Jo said. "But you played good baseball anyhow. You said you did."

"Well, that's so. But I had to fight it all the time. I kicked my mitt thirty yards!" Laughing, Andrew clutched his uncle's arm. "And I threw a great pass to first base!"

"You don't need Jo—you need a dictionary," said Uncle Donald.

"And you need to step out," Jo said. "You can't just lean against walls and wait to be asked."

"I know. I will try, Jo." Andrew really meant that. "I promise," he added. "But—do you want to go?"

Jo grabbed Andrew's pinky and squeezed it.

"You've been my good friend," he said. "I always wanted a friend. But Andrew, you live in Ohio. Your uncle roams about and someday, he says, he will take me home. You see?"

"I see." Andrew wiped his glasses clean. "Home is clear across the ocean, I suppose. But if Uncle Donald says he will take you home, he will. Hop in the bottle, then."

Andrew looked at his uncle. "You better not be careless, though. Don't lose him."

"I promise," said Uncle Donald.

He held out the polish bottle, and Jo, with a wink at Andrew, disappeared inside. Uncle Donald put the top on, tight.

"Thank you, Andrew," he said. "Now look, I know

you'll miss Jo. He's a good fellow, but maybe this will help. There must be something you need." He gave Andrew the peanut-butter jar now filled with folded green stuff, and headed down the stairs.

The only thing I need is Jo—no more, no less, thought Andrew. He watched his uncle stride across the school yard below the window, and thought some more.

Then Mrs. Carson came by on the way to the lunchroom. She pointed to the end of the line, behind Billy and Kevin, and Andrew followed.

There he took a deep breath. "Listen, Kevin, I like insects okay too. Maybe we could work on something this summer. Plant tomatoes and grow our own bugs. Together, I mean. Both of us."

Kevin shrugged and grinned, but before he answered, Andrew took another deep breath and added, "Could I play ball with you guys tomorrow? I'm not good, but maybe I could get better."

"You weren't so bad. Why not play today?" asked Kevin.

"I can't." Andrew slid the folded green money out of the jar and stuck it in his pocket. He dropped the jar into the wastebasket. "I have to go and buy a purple watch," he said.